R0083488262

09/2015

PALM BEACH COUNTY
LIBRARY SYSTEM
3650 Summit Boulevard
West Palm Beach. FL 33406-4198

SCOOBY-DOO!
SUPER SPOOKY
DOUBLE STORYBOOK

Written by Jesse Leon McCann
Illustrated by Duendes del Sur

ISBN 13: 978-0-545-03153-0
ISBN 10: 0-545-03153-2
Compilation Copyright © 2008 by Hanna-Barbera
Scooby-Doo and the Werewolf © 2004 by Hanna-Barbera
Scooby-Doo and the Tiki's Curse © 2004 by Hanna-Barbera
SCOOBY-DOO and all related characters and elements are trademarks of and © Hanna-Barbera.
Published by Scholastic Inc. All rights reserved. SCHOLASTIC and associated logos are trademarks and/or registered trademarks of Scholastic Inc.

12 11   13 14 15 16/0
                                                    40
Printed in the U.S.A.
First printing, January 2008

SCHOLASTIC INC.
New York Toronto London Auckland Sydney
Mexico City New Delhi Hong Kong Buenos Aires

For Danielle and Ashley: Love ya, girls!

There was lots of excitement at Shaggy's house! An exchange student from Romania was coming to stay with Shaggy and Scooby-Doo. They didn't know anything about Romania, so Velma brought over some books for them to read.

3

"Zoinks!" cried Shaggy after Velma left. "That's a lot of books! Like, I've got a better idea, Scoob. Let's rent a video about Romania instead."

"Reah! Reah!" Scooby agreed. He licked his chops. Now he and Shaggy could eat popcorn and snacks and learn at the same time!

The movie the two friends rented told the story of a young man from Romania who was cursed by a gypsy. Every time the autumn moon rose, he would turn into a werewolf! The movie had a lot of spooky special effects. It was very scary!

ARRIVALS ▷ GATE 2

The next day, the Mystery, Inc. gang went to the airport to pick up André, the Romanian exchange student. Shaggy and Scooby were a little nervous about André staying with them. After all, Romania was where werewolves came from!

When André got off the plane, Scooby-Doo and Shaggy turned cold with fear.

"Like, gee whiz, Scooby," Shaggy gulped. "Look how hairy André is!"

"Reah!" Scooby shivered. "Rairy rike a rererolf!"

Shaggy and Scooby-Doo worried all day long. What would happen after sunset, when the moon came out? It was September, an autumn moon. Fortunately, André retired to his room as soon as evening fell. Unfortunately, they found animal hairs all over the house! Were they from André?

Scooby and Shaggy couldn't sleep. Not when a werewolf might be staying in their house! They kept guard until midnight. Then they heard someone open and close the front door. It was André! He'd sneaked outside in the middle of the night!

"Zoinks! He's howling at the moon, Scoob!" Shaggy whispered urgently. "And he's all hairy!"

"Roh ro!" Scooby was about to faint.

Scooby and Shaggy raced back home and hid under Shaggy's bed. They couldn't sleep a wink! Had André really turned into a werewolf?

Scooby and Shaggy knew they had to find out for sure. First
thing in the morning, they went to an old bookstore. Way in
the back were all the books about monsters. Shaggy read about
werewolves — most important, how to tell if someone is one!

One book Shaggy read said that werewolves are driven away by a plant called wolfsbane. Luckily, there was a shop in town that sold it. Scooby and Shaggy took the wolfsbane home and showed it to André. André quickly excused himself and left the room!

Another book said that werewolves didn't like things made of silver. So Shaggy grabbed a silver spoon from the kitchen. When André wasn't expecting it, Shaggy and Scooby jumped out and held up the spoon. Sure enough, André turned away. Now they were certain that André was a werewolf!

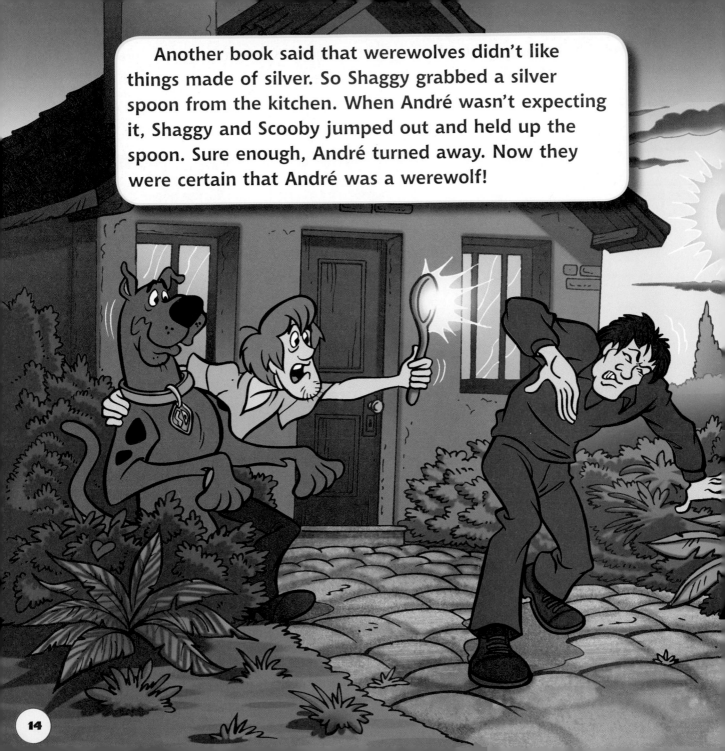

Shaggy and Scooby needed to warn their friends. They knew Velma and Daphne would be over at Fred's house. As soon as André was out of the way, they slipped out. But they had a funny feeling they were being followed! Was it André?

Scooby and Shaggy dashed through the baseball field and vacant lots, through the park and into back alleys. They were certain André was right behind them — and he was probably gaining on them!

Just when they thought they couldn't take another step, Shaggy pulled Scooby behind some trash cans. The creature behind them passed by without noticing them.

"Zoinks! That was close!" Shaggy panted. "C'mon, Scoob! Let's get to Fred's!"

"Relp! Relp! Rerewolf!" Scooby-Doo cried as he and Shaggy charged into Fred's house.

"Like, you've got to help us!" Shaggy hollered. "The werewolf may be right outside!"

"Jinkies! What are you guys talking about?" Velma frowned. "There's no such thing as werewolves!"

Just then, André walked out of the rest room.
"Like, it's him!" Shaggy shrieked. "He's the werewolf!"
"We invited André over for a nice dinner, not to be called a werewolf," Daphne said.

"Oh yeah?" Shaggy said. "If he's not a werewolf, then why did he turn furry and howl at the moon? Why did he leave hairs all over the house? And why did he run away when we brought out wolfsbane and silver? Huh? Huh?"

"Reah!" Scooby scowled suspiciously.

"I am so sorry," André said shyly. "My fur coat is getting very old. I am afraid it sheds."

"I howled at the moon because I was so very happy to be spending time in America, you see," André explained. "But I do not understand your customs here. Why did you wave weeds in my face? I am very allergic. And why did you use that spoon to reflect sunlight at me? It really hurt my eyes!"

"Like . . . because . . . uh . . . you're a . . . werewolf?" Shaggy said timidly.

"Whew! Sorry, André. Like, Scooby and I feel like first-class dunces!" Shaggy sighed. "Right, Scoob?"

"Ruh-huh!" Scooby agreed.

"It is funny you thought I was a werewolf." André smiled. "Yet you never asked which part of Romania I am from."

"I am from Transylvania!" André declared. "Home of the vampire!"

For a second, Shaggy and Scooby were scared stiff! Then they heard their friends laughing, and they knew André was just kidding. Soon everyone was laughing, cheering, and giving André a proper welcome.

"Scooby-Dooby-Doo!" Scooby exclaimed.

Scooby and his Mystery, Inc. friends were visiting Hawaii. They were planning to ride their bikes in a race for charity. They were also planning to have some fun!

Sand surfing over the black sands of Oneuli Beach was a *whole* lot of fun!

"Roo hoo!" Scooby-Doo rode the wind, major kine style!

"The sand pebbles are made of black lava basalt," Velma explained. "It reflects the sun, so put on your sunblock!"

29

Suddenly, the wind blew! The water churned!
A huge, fearsome statue rose out of the water!

30

"Leave this place!" the statue boomed. "I, tiki god Pu'u Ola'i, demand it!"

Spitting fire, the tiki drew nearer. Everyone ran away as fast as they could!

Afterward, the gang wondered what the tiki was, and why it wanted everyone off the beach.

"Pu'u Ola'i doesn't just want everyone to leave the beach," said an eavesdropping old woman. "The legend says that it wants all strangers to leave Maui forever!"

Later, their host, Johnny Kopono, drove the kids up the Hana Highway.

Johnny pointed to a man passing them at a dangerous speed. "That babooze is Cedric Pennington, the millionaire. He wants to buy my family's land, but we won't sell."

33

Johnny took them to the Seven Sacred Pools, one of the most beautiful spots in Hawaii.

34

"Like, this is what I call living!" Shaggy exclaimed. "The only thing missing is a luau!"

"Reah! Reah!" Scooby-Doo licked his lips hungrily.

But the angry monster tiki suddenly appeared, just as it had done on the beach.

"You will be destroyed!" the tiki bellowed. "You will feel my wrath!"

Shaggy and Scooby ran as fast as they could from the creepy tiki! They raced away from the pools and across a nearby pasture. The tiki chased them. "Doom! Doom!" it shouted.

"Zoinks!" yelled Shaggy.

"Relp! Relp!" cried Scooby.

That evening, the gang sat down to talk. "I know this tiki is a fake," Fred said. "Come on, gang! Let's solve this mystery!"

The kids went hiking around the area where they'd seen the tiki. Velma thought she'd spotted a clue, but when they got closer, there was nothing there.

The next morning, it was time for the big charity bicycle race. The Mystery, Inc. gang forgot about the tiki menace and got ready for some serious fun!

Snobby Cedric Pennington wasn't having fun, though. Johnny still wouldn't sell his land.

"Like, faster, Scooby, we're in last place," Shaggy huffed. "Maybe we shouldn't have eaten those thirty pineapple-chili burgers until after the race!"

"Ruh-huh!" Scooby puffed.

But then the tiki appeared once more. "Doom! Doom on you!"
it boomed.

"Look out!" Fred warned, but it was too late. The cyclists
crashed their bikes!

"Jeepers!" cried Daphne.

Scooby and Shaggy cycled right through the tiki, off the road and into the ocean. SPLASH!

And just as suddenly as it had appeared, the tiki disappeared.

"Jinkies!" Velma exclaimed. She had seen something unusual. But when she blinked and looked again, it was gone.

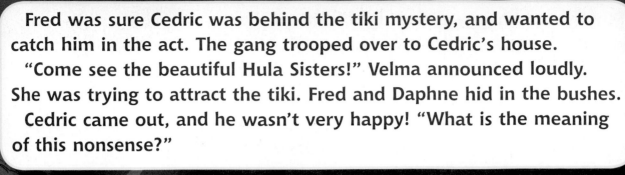

Fred was sure Cedric was behind the tiki mystery, and wanted to catch him in the act. The gang trooped over to Cedric's house.

"Come see the beautiful Hula Sisters!" Velma announced loudly. She was trying to attract the tiki. Fred and Daphne hid in the bushes.

Cedric came out, and he wasn't very happy! "What is the meaning of this nonsense?"

Just then, the terrifying tiki appeared again. "You have been warned! Now you must pay!"

It was clear that Cedric wasn't behind it after all. When he saw the tiki, he shrieked and ran away!

A sudden light came from above. The whole area lit up. The tiki became a harmless illusion projected upon flying grains of black sand. Their friend Johnny Kopono had solved the mystery!

"Curse you meddling kids and your nosy dog!" screeched the old woman. "We wanted to frighten everyone away! Then we could have bought this land for next to nothing!"

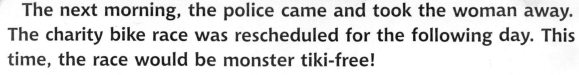

The next morning, the police came and took the woman away. The charity bike race was rescheduled for the following day. This time, the race would be monster tiki-free!

"Like, now it's time for more fun in the sun!" Shaggy grinned. "Right, Scoob?"

"Right!" agreed Scooby-Doo. "Aloha-rooby-dooby-doo!"